MW01013097

Sparrow Jack

MORDICAI GERSTEIN

FRANCES FOSTER BOOKS
FARRAR, STRAUS AND GIROUX
NEW YORK

MONMOUTH COUNTY LIBRARY
EASTERN BRANCH

With thanks to all the birds
who share this world with us
so cheerfully

Copyright © 2003 by Mordicai Gerstein
All rights reserved
Distributed in Canada by Douglas & McIntyre Ltd.
Color separations by Hong Kong Scanner Arts
Printed and bound in the United States of America by Phoenix Color Corporation
Designed by Barbara Grzeslo
First edition, 2003
1 3 5 7 9 10 8 6 4 2

Library of Congress Cataloging-in-Publication Data
Gerstein, Mordicai.
Sparrow Jack / Mordicai Gerstein— 1st ed.
    p. cm.
    Summary: In 1868, John Bardsley, an immigrant from England, brought one thousand
sparrows from his home country back to Philadelphia, where he hoped they would help
save the trees from the inch-worms that were destroying them. Based on a true story.
    ISBN 0-374-37139-3
    1. Bardsley, John—Juvenile fiction. [1. Bardsley, John—Fiction. 2. Sparrows—Fiction.
3. Immigrants—Fiction. 4. Philadelphia (Pa.)—History—Fiction. 5. Pennsylvania—History—
1865–-Fiction.] I. Title.

PZ7.G325 Sp 2003
[E]—dc21

                                                                              2001023829

Foreword

Not all the immigrants that came to America in the early days were people. French dogs, Siamese cats, English cows, Icelandic sheep, and many other animals were brought over to do jobs that native animals couldn't do.

Few people know that the common house sparrow, the noisy little brown birds seen everywhere, didn't get to America until 1868, when a thousand of them were brought from England to do a special job. This is the story—pieced together from scraps of history, old news clippings, and bits of sparrow legend and gossip—of how these lively, raucous birds became Americans.

Young John Bardsley tiptoed into the English twilight to catch a dozen sleeping sparrows for dinner. It was 1838, and people thought sparrows were greedy, noisy pests, but tasty snacks when roasted.

John heard a "SQUEAK! SQUEAK!" underfoot. A baby sparrow had fallen from its nest.

"HUNGRY! HUNGRY!" it seemed to say.

"Poor little thing," said John, and picked it up. Instead of killing it, he took it home.

John fed it worms and grubs. Hundreds of them! How could
something so tiny eat so much, and chirp for more? The
sparrow washed with him, slept with him, and rode around on
his hat. It was cheerful, brave, and loyal. After it rejoined its
flock, it still came to visit, and brought its brothers, sisters, aunts,
uncles, cousins, and friends. John never hunted another
sparrow.

When John grew up, he decided to seek his fortune in America. Jobs and money were scarce in England. A flock of sparrows came to his ship to say goodbye. "Will there be sparrows in America?" he wondered. It was a long, stormy voyage and John was seasick all the way.

There were no sparrows in America, and John missed them. But there was plenty of work. John became a house painter.

One spring morning in 1868, he was painting his own little house in Philadelphia. Something tickly fell down his back. It made him itch. Then it made him wiggle and twitch.

He fell off his ladder. Fortunately, he wasn't hurt. An inchworm had fallen into his shirt. He looked around and saw inchworms everywhere.

They were eating the leaves off all the trees and bushes, and falling down the backs of all the people of Philadelphia, making them all wiggle and twitch.

As the inchworms ate the leaves, the trees and bushes of Philadelphia began to die. The birds of Philadelphia—jays, wrens, robins, and thrushes—just turned up their beaks at the inchworms. They wouldn't eat them.

The city council hired a small army of men and children to pick the inchworms off the trees. But no matter how many they picked, there were always ten times more left. No one knew what to do.

John Bardsley sat under his dying trees and tried to think of an answer. A squeaky wagon passed. The sound reminded him of something. What was it? Of course! The squeak of a baby sparrow! That was the answer! Bring sparrows to America to eat the inchworms. They would eat anything, and lots of it!

Bardsley ran to the city council to get money for his idea.

"Can you promise," they asked, "that English birds will eat American worms?"

"I think they will," he said. "But I can't promise."

"Sorry," they said, and turned him down.

Bardsley decided to set off on his own. It was a long, stormy voyage. He was seasick all the way.

    In his hometown of Ashton, England, everyone laughed when they heard why he'd come.

    "A thousand sparrows?" giggled his parents, aunts, uncles, and cousins. "Please, take two thousand!"

    "Take them all!" insisted his sisters.

    "Thank you," he said, "but one thousand should do the trick."

Then he went to tell the sparrows his plan.

"Dear friends, I've missed you," he said, sitting under a tree where they fluttered and chirped. "There's work for you in America. You'll be appreciated and respected. Philadelphians don't eat sparrows."

He listened to the chirping overhead and fell into a kind of doze.

Did he really hear the sparrows speaking? Or was it a dream?

"He wants us to leave our homes and families," some seemed to chirp.

"America's too far!" others worried. "We could never fly back."

"What do they have to eat over there?" asked a hungry nestling.

"Quiet, all of you!" chirped the sparrow chief. "Face facts. We're despised and hunted here. They hate us!"

"It's true, it's true," chirped the flock.

"In America, we'd be needed," said the chief. "And we'd
have all the inchworms we could swallow!"

"What're inchworms?" chirped a little chirper.

"They're small," said his mother, "but tasty."

"All right!" crowed the chief. "We need one thousand
hungry sparrows. Who's willing to go?"

One thousand sparrows chirped at once, and all over
Ashton people jumped and dropped things.

Bardsley leaped to his feet, wide awake. "What a dream!"
he said.

That evening, when Bardsley and the town children went
out to catch the birds, one thousand sparrows flew into the nets.

They were put in little reed cages and taken by wagon to
Liverpool. A cloud of sparrows flew along to wish them luck.

"Amazing," said people at the dock as the caged birds were
loaded onto the ship and their relatives chirped, "Goodbye!"

Despite a long, stormy voyage, the sparrows were cheerful.
John Bardsley was seasick all the way.

There was no brass band to meet them on the cold, gray rainy day they landed in America. John protected the birds with his umbrella while they waited for a wagon. He got soaked, and caught a cold.

All through the winter, Bardsley kept one thousand sparrows snug and warm in his house.

"All right!" Bardsley said to the birds on the first day of
spring. "Show them what a sparrow can do!" And he released
them.

Everyone in Philadelphia watched to see what would
happen.

As the inchworms crawled up the trees, the sparrows
built nests. They laid eggs while the inchworms began eating
the new leaves.

"They're worthless!" wailed the people of Philadelphia.
The sparrows sat on their eggs and ignored the worms.

Then the baby sparrows hatched, squeaking, "HUNGRY!
HUNGRY!" Their parents flew out and began collecting
inchworms by the thousands and stuffing them into their chicks.
"Amazing!" cried the people of Philadelphia.

They watched the inchworms disappear. Everyone was
happy: the sparrows, the Philadelphians, and, of course, John
Bardsley, who from then on was called Sparrow Jack. He liked
the name.

Philadelphia was never again bothered by inchworms, but many people began complaining about "those noisy little pests, the sparrows!"

The sparrows didn't mind, and neither did John Bardsley. He had his sparrow friends around him again. And for him, they were very good friends indeed.